# I'm Sorry

*For Dylan and Megan* – J.E.

First published in hardback by HarperCollins*Publishers* Ltd in 2000
First published in paperback in Great Britain by Collins Picture Books in 2001

3 5 7 9 10 8 6 4 2

ISBN: 978-0-00-780015-5

Collins Picture Books is an imprint of the Children's Division, part of HarperCollins Publishers Ltd.
Text copyright © Sam McBratney 2000
Illustrations copyright © Jennifer Eachus 2000

Visit our website at: www.harpercollinschildrensbooks.co.uk

Printed in China

# I'm Sorry

## Sam McBratney

*illustrated by* Jennifer Eachus

HarperCollins *Children's Books*

I have a friend I love the best.

I have a friend I love the best.

She plays at my house every day,
or else I play at hers.

I have a friend I love the best.
I think she's nice.

The things we do
always make me laugh,
and she thinks I'm nice, too.

She lets me be the teacher
when we teach our
toys to read...

...I let her be the doctor
and fix my bones.

We make her baby smile
when he wakes up
from his sleep...

...And sometimes we
put our wellies on

to see how deep
the puddles are.

I have a friend I love the best.
I think she's nice.

The things we do
always make me laugh,
and she thinks I'm nice, too.
But...

# I SHOUTED at my friend today,

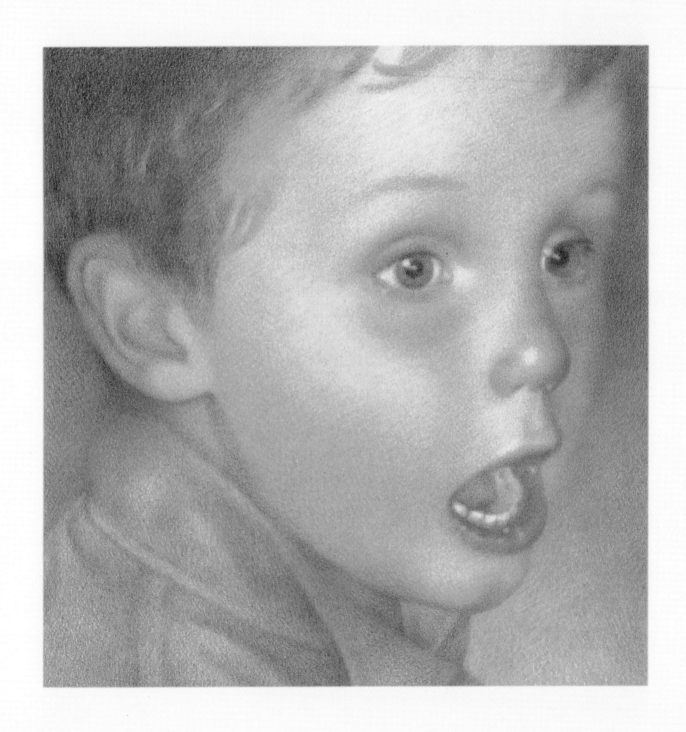

and she shouted back at me.

I wouldn't speak to
her any more, and
she won't speak to me.

My friend shouted at me today,
and I shouted back at her.
She wouldn't play with me any more,
and I won't play with her.

I pretend my friend's not there,

and she pretends she doesn't care, but...

I do care.

If my friend was as
sad as I am sad, this
is what she would do:

she would come and say, "I'm sorry,"

and I would say sorry, too.